Juliet
the Valentine Fairy

To Amy, who inspires all kinds of love.

Special thanks to
Kristin Earhart

ISBN-10: 0-545-14886-3
ISBN-13: 978-0-545-14886-3

20 19 18 17 16   18/0
Printed in the U.S.A.

First printing, December 2009

Juliet
the Valentine
Fairy

by Daisy Meadows

SCHOLASTIC INC.

New York   Toronto   London   Auckland
Sydney   Mexico City   New Delhi   Hong Kong

The Fairyland Palace

The Florist

Wetherbury Village

Greenhouse

Juliet's Cottage

Jack Frost's Ice Castle

Town Square

Kirsty's House

Darden Hall

Art Center

Card-Making Mishap

It's Valentine's Day and love is everywhere,
but I, Jack Frost, feel it isn't fair.
Friends and families and sweethearts, too,
I've got a mean surprise for you.

This holiday is no longer nice.
If you celebrate, you will pay the price.
Giving cards and gifts is a big mistake,
These things will cause your hearts to break.

**Find the hidden letters in the hearts throughout
this book. Unscramble all 6 letters to spell
a special Valentine phrase!**

Contents

Late for a Date

Kirsty Tate paced from the front hall to
the kitchen and back again. She pulled
aside the curtain and looked out the
window. There was still no sign of her
best friend, Rachel Walker. Kirsty
glanced at the grandfather clock in the
corner and sighed. The Valentine's card

workshop had already started. Why was Rachel so late? Kirsty stared out the window, hoping the Walkers' familiar station wagon would magically appear — but she knew that she couldn't just make magic happen. The truth was, she and Rachel knew a lot about magic! They had learned about it from their good friends, the fairies.

The two girls had first met on a trip to Rainspell Island. There, they helped the seven Rainbow Fairies, who had been sent away from Fairyland by the wicked Jack Frost. Rachel and Kirsty made a great team. The king and queen of Fairyland came to rely on the girls whenever Jack Frost and his goblins were causing trouble.

Kirsty was happy that the fairies could trust them, and she knew she could trust Rachel, too. She couldn't help smiling when she spotted the station wagon turning down her street.

As the car pulled into the Tates' driveway, Rachel waved cheerfully to Kirsty, who hurried out to help with her friend's bag. Rachel kissed her mom good-bye.

"Hello, Kirsty!" Mrs. Walker said. She turned back to her daughter. "Rachel, please call and let me know what time I should pick you up on Sunday." Rachel nodded and waved as her mom drove off.

"I'm so glad you're here," Kirsty said, hugging her best friend. "I was starting to worry." Rachel frowned and tilted her head to the side. "We'll just put your bag in my room and go straight to the Art Center," Kirsty continued.

"But I thought the Valentine workshop was after dinner," Rachel said, looking confused.

"No," Kirsty replied. She couldn't help feeling a little annoyed. "But we should still have time," she added hopefully. "Let's tell my dad we're ready to go."

The two friends dropped Rachel's bag upstairs and headed to the kitchen. Through the window over the sink, they could see Kirsty's father working in the backyard. Kirsty poked her head out the

back door. "Dad, can you take us to the Art Center now?" she asked. "Rachel's here." Mr. Tate looked up from a pile of wood and chicken wire. "Hi, Rachel!" he called. Then he wiped his forehead with his sleeve and looked at Kirsty. "I completely forgot that I was supposed to take you girls to the class. It's so nice out. I started making the new compost bin for your mom." He glanced down at the pile of building supplies and furrowed his brow. "I still have a lot to do, and I've made a big mess. Do you think you girls could ride bikes to the Art Center?"

Kirsty felt a frown tug at the corners of her mouth. She had left her dad a note. Why did he forget? And how would she ever make a Valentine's card with so little time? She wanted to be angry with him, but then she looked at the blue sky and sighed. "It *is* very nice out for February," she admitted.

Rachel nodded in agreement.

"I'll pick you up afterward, and we'll put the bikes in the trunk," Mr. Tate said.

"Okay — the workshop is over at 6:30," replied Kirsty. "See you then!"

Mr. Tate gave his daughter a warm smile

and watched as she grabbed her friend's hand and ran back inside the house.

"You can ride my new bike," Kirsty offered as they skipped down the garage steps. She pointed to a purple road bike with a green straw basket on the front. Once Rachel swung her leg over the bar and had one foot on a pedal, Kirsty grabbed the handlebars of a yellow bike with pink flowers on it. "This one was my cousin's. It's a little small, but I can still ride it," Kirsty said. She grinned. "And I bet I can beat you there!"

Workshop Woes

After a quick ride into Wetherbury Village, Kirsty and Rachel turned off the sidewalk and into the Art Center parking lot. Like many of the older buildings at Wetherbury College, the Art Center had a slate roof and stained-glass windows.

"It's beautiful," Rachel said, climbing off her bike.

"Our class is on the third floor," Kirsty
said, turning the key on her bike lock.
The girls ran up the stairs to the
classroom.

A tall man with a shaggy red beard
greeted them. "Hello, Kirsty," he said.
"And you must be Rachel." The man
nodded as he marked their names on
his clipboard.

"Hello, Mr. Snouffer,"
Kirsty said. "I'm sorry
we're late."

Mr. Snouffer shook his
head. "No worries, dear.
All the art supplies are
out on the tables," he
said. "You still have
plenty of time to make something from
the heart."

Kirsty and Rachel looked at each
other, trying not to giggle.

"Oh, my!" Mr. Snouffer chuckled, looking around at all the hearts on the other kids' Valentines cards. "From the *heart*. That's funny."

"Yes," Kirsty said, giggling. "It *is* funny." Then she walked to a table with two open seats and picked out some paper and markers. She turned to Rachel. "I want to make my parents a special card. They do so much for me,

and I thought it would be nice to say
thanks!"

"Yeah, except your
dad wouldn't drive us
here," Rachel
mumbled. Her
eyebrows shot
up as she
glanced over at
Kirsty. Her friend was
just as surprised as Rachel was that
she had said that! "I'm sorry, Kirsty,"
Rachel gasped. "I really didn't mean it
that way."

Kirsty nodded and bit her lip. She had
been annoyed with her dad, too, but she
didn't like to hear her friend criticizing
him. She didn't say anything, though,
and went back to making her card.

At the next table, two friends began arguing loudly. "You're copying me," declared a girl with short brown hair.

"I was using the star stickers first!" the other girl replied.

"No, you weren't." The two girls scowled at each other until one pushed her chair back loudly and stood up. "Fine, I'm changing tables," she huffed, heading off to find a new seat.

Almost immediately, Kirsty and Rachel
heard another disagreement coming from
a different table. "Stop kicking me!" A
boy's voice carried across the room.

"Jackson? Andrew? What seems to be
the problem?" Mr. Snouffer asked.

Kirsty glanced over and saw two boys
from her school giving each other icy
stares. "They're best friends," Kirsty
whispered to Rachel in shock. "They
never fight."

The girls locked eyes. "Do you think something funny is going on?" Rachel asked.

"It seems that way," Kirsty answered, raising an eyebrow.

"You're right!" a tiny voice sang out so only Rachel and Kirsty could hear.

"What?" Rachel and Kirsty both said, each glancing at the other.

"You're right," the small, sweet voice said again. "Something funny is going on." After a pause, the voice became serious. "Well, it's actually not funny at all."

The two girls peered around the room until their eyes fell upon a fairy! She was so small that she was hiding in

a glass jar of glitter, right in front of them on the table.

"Oh, hello!" Rachel gasped. Kirsty immediately folded a large piece of construction paper and propped it up on the table, so no one else could see their fairy friend.

As soon as the coast was clear, the fairy fluttered out of the jar. She unfolded her wings, and a mix of craft sparkles and

magical heart
sparkles swirled
around her. Her
long, brown hair
fell in waves past
her shoulders, and
she wore a wide-
necked pink
sweater and a
jean skirt with two hearts stitched to the
front. Her beaded necklace had a red
heart pendant.

But more than anything, Kirsty and
Rachel noticed the pretty fairy's deep,
brown eyes — which were brimming
with tears.

Juliet's Story

"Kirsty and Rachel," the fairy said, sighing. "I'm so lucky I found you! It's the only good thing that's happened all day." A single tear ran down one of her rosy cheeks.

Kirsty and Rachel looked at the little fairy with concern.

"Oh, please forgive me," the fairy said, perking up a bit. "I know your names, but you don't know mine!" She brushed the extra sparkles from her skirt and bent her knees in a little curtsy. "I'm  Juliet the Valentine Fairy. It's my job to make sure that Valentine's Day is full of love and happiness, both in Fairyland and the human world. But I'm afraid I've messed up everything this year!"

"Oh, Juliet. I'm sure it's not that bad," Rachel said, trying to reassure the fairy.

"Oh, but it is." Juliet's tone was very dramatic. "Friends and families are fighting. Sweethearts are falling out of love. People are not thinking about one another's feelings." She pulled out a pink tissue and sniffled. "Everything that makes Valentine's Day special is coming apart!" She buried her face in her hands.

"Tell us what happened," Kirsty suggested. "Maybe we can help."

Juliet raised her head. "I was finishing making this year's Valentines when I heard some beautiful music. I went outside to see where it was coming from, but no one was there. When I went back into my cottage, I discovered that all three of my magical Valentine's Day presents were gone!" The fairy's shoulders slumped. Kirsty and Rachel

could see that it was hard for her to tell the story.

"I grabbed my wand and raced out the back door. A band of goblins was running down the lane! I tried to stop them, but I couldn't cast a spell because my fingers were still too sticky from the glue I'd used. As soon as I got a good grip on my wand, the spell came

barreling out. But just then, Jack Frost appeared — and he cast a spell that rocketed straight at mine! The two spells collided and spun into a whirlwind of magic . . . right above the goblins." Juliet twirled her hands around, mimicking the magical storm. "Now my presents are lost somewhere in the human world. If I don't find them and return them to Fairyland, Valentine's Day won't be the same."

"What happens if you don't get the presents back?" Rachel asked.

"Jack Frost's spell ensures that every card or present will have the opposite effect of what it should." Juliet shook her head in disbelief. "And this time, he's given the goblins a wand that can mix up messages. They're using it to change the meanings of e-mails and notes. It's a mess!"

Kirsty and Rachel felt their hearts sink. They had already seen what could happen! Friends were fighting, and Kirsty thought about how she had been annoyed with her dad. Normally, she would have been more understanding.

"You both need to know this," Juliet announced seriously. "The three missing presents stand for three kinds of love. First, the Valentine's card represents family love. Second," the fairy said, counting on her fingers, "is the red rose. It stands for sweetheart love. And the final present is the box of super-sweet

candy hearts. Those
are for friendship,
of course. Each
present is tied with
a sparkly red ribbon."

Both girls thought of
all the special kinds of love. They
couldn't let them be ruined! "We have
to do something!" declared Rachel.

"I would love your help," Juliet replied,
giving the girls a tiny smile. "But we
have to let the magic come to us, you
know. Let's be on the lookout. Jack Frost
told his goblins to do whatever they had
to so that we wouldn't get the magical
presents back."

Kirsty nodded, remembering how
Fairyland magic worked. The presents

needed to be back in Fairyland before
the holiday would be magical again!

"I guess you girls should just work on
your Valentines for now," Juliet said,
shrugging. "At least until we find a
clue . . . or until the goblins find us."

No-Good Goblins

Kirsty took Juliet's advice and immediately went back to making her Valentine. She wasn't ready for a fairy adventure yet — she still had to finish her parents' card! She reached in front of Rachel to grab more pipe cleaners and tissue paper.

Rachel frowned as Kirsty picked out the art supplies. She couldn't understand why her friend wasn't more worried about the missing presents. Didn't she care? "Why are you even bothering with that silly card?" Rachel asked. "If we don't hurry up and find Juliet's presents, it won't matter if you finish it or not."

Kirsty's jaw dropped, and her eyes narrowed. "If you hadn't been so late, I wouldn't have to hurry," she replied quietly. "Oh, girls, please

don't argue!" pleaded Juliet. "Jack Frost's magic will work against you two, since you're best friends. You might say and do things you normally wouldn't — all because the Valentine presents are missing!"

Kirsty and Rachel both looked down. They were embarrassed. Of course, Juliet was right. An upbeat attitude was the way to get the best of the goblins. They couldn't let silly arguments stop them!

"I want some more decorations for my card," Kirsty suddenly announced, studying her Valentine. She stood up and walked over to Mr. Snouffer's desk.

Immediately, Juliet flitted to Rachel's shoulder. "We should follow her," whispered the fairy. "It's best to stick together." Rachel quickly stood up, and Juliet fluttered to her shoulder, to hide behind her hair. Rachel was relieved to be doing something other than arts and crafts, but she *really* wanted to be tracking down those no-good goblins!

"Why, Kirsty," Mr. Snouffer said, "your card is lovely."

"Thank you," replied Kirsty. She'd done a lot of work on her card so far. The front had delicate tissue-paper flowers clustered into the shape of a heart, and drizzled with red and pink glitter. Inside, she had written a poem to her parents. It was a very pretty card, but Kirsty couldn't help feeling like something was missing. "I was hoping to add a little something else," she explained to her teacher. "Do you have any scraps of ribbon or paper from our project last week?"

"Oh yes," said Mr. Snouffer with an understanding smile. "You'll find what

you're looking for in the scrap bin in
the hall closet."

Kirsty grinned and headed across the
room and out the door. Rachel followed
just a few steps behind. "Wait, Kirsty!"
she called, but her friend didn't hear.

Rachel stepped into the hallway just as
Kirsty opened the supply closet door. At
once, a big box of art supplies fell on

Kirsty's head — and two goblins tumbled out of the closet! Rachel noticed that one goblin clutched a pink card with a sparkly red ribbon looped around it. The other goblin held a long, skinny wand.

As the goblins scrambled to their feet, Rachel rushed forward to help her friend.

"My card!" Juliet cried, pointing from her perch on Rachel's shoulder. "That goblin has it!"

As Rachel lifted the box off Kirsty's head, colorful fabric and paper scraps fell to the ground. "Are you okay?" she asked, worried.

"Yes — let's catch those goblins!" Kirsty cried. As the

girls ran down the hallway, Juliet peeked
over Rachel's shoulder and twirled her
wand. Magically, the box of art
materials floated back into the closet
with the paper and fabric scraps safely
inside.

"The goblins are fast!" Rachel yelled,
stumbling down the Art Center stairs.
The heavy main door scraped open
when Kirsty pushed it.

The sky was growing dark as the sun set. The girls searched the campus sidewalks for the goblins, but they could not even hear any footsteps. It was almost like the goblins had simply disappeared!

"But they had my Valentine's Day card! What will we do now?" asked Juliet.

A Simple Swap

"Don't worry, Juliet," Rachel said. "We'll help get your card back."

"That's right," agreed Kirsty, walking up to a large map of the campus. "Maybe this will give us an idea of where the goblins went."

"It can give us more than an idea!" Juliet cried, flying off of Rachel's

shoulder. "I think this map can tell us *exactly* where to find them." She straightened her skirt and lifted her wand. "Little hearts, be our guide, show us where the goblins hide." A cluster of heart sparkles burst out of Juliet's wand and whizzed straight to the map, landing on DARDEN HALL.

"Darden Hall is a small, old theater," Kirsty said. "It's right over there."

Juliet followed Kirsty's gaze and immediately  flew toward the tall, brick building. The girls ran behind her, right up the front steps. The carved wooden door creaked

as Kirsty pulled it open. At once, the
three friends could hear the two goblins'
voices — arguing! They were standing at
the front of the theater on a small stage.
Juliet and the girls snuck inside and
peeked out from behind the last row of
red cushioned seats.

"Why did you mix up the message on
the card?" asked the goblin with big feet.

"Jack Frost told us to mix up all
messages, especially Valentines," the
other goblin grumbled.

"Well, we can't read it, so we don't know if it's real. We can't take it to Jack Frost like this!" The first goblin pouted. "It doesn't even have a sparkly red ribbon."

Juliet, Rachel, and Kirsty looked at one another with wide eyes. The goblins didn't know that they had the real magical card!

Rachel leaned in to her friends and spoke as quietly as she could. "I think we would have spotted the ribbon if it had fallen off on the way here."

"So the ribbon is probably somewhere in the theater," Kirsty mused. The girls peered over the chairs and peeked down the aisle, searching for the ribbon.

Juliet flitted into the air for a fairy's-eye view, being careful to stay out of sight of the goblins. With an excited twirl, she swooped down behind a row of seats. When the  fairy reappeared, the red ribbon trailed behind her in the air.

Kirsty had to remind herself not to cheer out loud when Juliet dropped the ribbon safely in her lap. "Now we have the ribbon," she whispered, "but we still don't have the card."

"We have *a* card, though," Rachel declared. "Pass me the ribbon." Kirsty placed the red ribbon in her friend's hand. "Now hold out the card you made for your parents."

Kirsty clenched the flowery card tightly. Even though they'd made a mad dash from the Art Center, she had managed to keep it crisp and clean.

"Oh, I don't know . . ." Juliet began, watching Kirsty's face carefully. It was clear how much Kirsty liked her card!

"It's okay," Kirsty said. "I trust Rachel." She handed the card over, and watched as her friend tied the red ribbon around it.

"Now, here's the plan," Rachel announced, her eyes sparkling. She explained how they would trick the goblins. "Kirsty, just follow my lead. And, Juliet, don't let them know you're here!"

The two friends snuck back to the entrance of the theater, unseen. Then they stood up and acted as if they had just walked in. Juliet hid on Rachel's shoulder again.

"We're so lucky that we found the magic card," Rachel said loudly, trying to get the goblins' attention. "Now we can just hide in this theater until we know the goblins are gone."

Kirsty could hardly breathe. Out of the corner of her eye, she watched as the goblins onstage listened to what Rachel had said. "Yes," she added. "Juliet will be so happy to have her card back."

"Oh, no you don't!" shouted the goblin holding the wand.

"That card is ours!" the other goblin yelled. "Quick! Do a spell!" He nudged his goblin friend.

The first goblin pointed his wand at
Kirsty's pretty card and chanted,
"Whatever leaves Fairyland
and ends up lost, should
always belong to
Jack Frost."

"That's a
horrible spell,"
the other
goblin
scoffed.
"It's too
short! It
won't work."

But suddenly,
the card floated out
of Rachel's hand and zipped through the
air toward the goblins.

"It's working!" they declared, jumping up and down and looking goofy. Juliet giggled as she kept her wand pointed at the card. It was Juliet's magic that was carrying the card to the goblins, not their silly spell. But the goblins thought they had snatched the magical card from the girls!

"No!" Rachel yelled. "I found it first!"
She raced toward the stage, pretending to
be very upset.

"It's ours," the big-footed goblin said,
holding the card tightly. "We get the
pretty magic card. You
can have this silly little
one." He threw the real
magic card at Rachel.
Then both goblins
yelped with glee as
they stumbled off
the stage and ran
out of the theater.
Rachel picked up
the card and
carried it back
down the aisle
to Juliet.

"Thank you so much, Rachel," Juliet said. "Your plan worked perfectly. I can take my card back to Fairyland! Now families everywhere can  enjoy Valentine's Day together. With a twirl of my wand, the message will no longer be mixed up." With that, she waved her wand and shrunk the card back to Fairyland size. The message on the front now read HAPPY VALENTINE'S!

Kirsty couldn't help smiling at their new fairy friend. She was thrilled that they had helped Juliet get her card back, but she felt a little disappointed that the goblins had taken her card. She'd just have to make another one!

"We just have two more presents to go!" Rachel said with a grin. "Don't worry, Juliet. We'll find them. No matter what."

Kirsty gave Juliet a big wave as the fairy disappeared in a beautiful burst of sparkly red hearts. Then Kirsty heard the honk of her family's car. She and Rachel

ran outside to see Mr. Tate pulling up nearby, in front of the Art Center.

Kirsty smiled at her dad as she went to unlock her bike. She was happy to see him, and even happier that she and Rachel had helped Juliet track down one of her missing Valentine's Day presents!

The Red Rose Romp

Contents

Morning Muffins

As soon as Kirsty woke up the next morning, she went to her desk. It was Valentine's Day! "I have to make a new Valentine," she murmured, opening a drawer and searching for a clean sheet of construction paper. Kirsty grumbled when she found only a plain white piece. She glanced over at her best friend,

Rachel Walker, who was still asleep on the trundle bed.

Kirsty couldn't help thinking about the fancy card she had made the day before. She and Rachel had tricked the goblins into thinking that her card was Juliet the Valentine Fairy's magic card. It had been a good plan, but Kirsty still wished she could have given her card to her parents. She had worked hard on it!

Luckily, she remembered most of the poem she had composed for her card. She wrote it  on a new sheet of paper and drew some hearts on the page. It was simple, but it would have to do.

"Hey," Rachel said, sitting up and stretching her arms over her head. "Happy Valentine's Day!"

"Same to you," Kirsty said, smiling. Rachel always woke up cheerful. It was one of Kirsty's favorite things about her best friend.

"We have a lot to do today," Rachel announced, getting up and sifting through her bag. "We should get going."

"First we need to have breakfast. My mom always does something fun for Valentine's Day. It's kind of silly, but sweet," Kirsty admitted.

Rachel shrugged. "Just as long as it doesn't take too long."

Kirsty frowned at her friend's hasty tone. Then she remembered Juliet's warning. Since Jack Frost and his goblins had stolen Juliet's magical Valentine treats, families, sweethearts, and friends everywhere weren't getting along. Even Rachel and Kirsty were affected, since they were best friends! They would have to make an extra effort to work together. Luckily, they'd been able to do that when they found the magic Valentine card the day before, and now family love had been fixed.

"Maybe we should try to find the box of candy hearts next," Kirsty offered. If they found the magic candy, then friendship would be safe from Jack Frost's evil spell — and Kirsty and Rachel's friendship would be back to normal!

"That sounds good." Rachel pulled on a red-and-white striped sweater. "I just have to brush my teeth and call my

parents to wish them a happy Valentine's Day. I'll meet you downstairs?"

Kirsty nodded and headed for the kitchen. The smell of cinnamon was already wafting up the stairs.

When Rachel walked in the kitchen a few minutes later, the room grew quiet. Mr. and Mrs. Tate both gave tight smiles. Rachel thought Kirsty looked relieved to see her.

"My mom made us heart-shaped muffins. Let's eat them on the way," Kirsty suggested quickly, gulping down her orange juice.

Rachel noticed that Kirsty's hands fumbled as she hurried to wrap the muffins in a napkin. "Thanks, Mom. We'll see you later," Kirsty called over her shoulder as she rushed out of the room.

Rachel gave a confused wave and followed her friend.

As soon as Rachel walked into the garage, Kirsty closed the door behind her. Kirsty's shoulders slumped as she let out a sigh. "My parents were fighting," she said. "It was something silly about my mom not liking where my dad put the compost bin. But they both seemed really upset." Kirsty looked into her friend's eyes. "Do you think it's because of Jack Frost?"

"Probably," Rachel assured her. "We still have to find the candy hearts *and* the red rose — friendship love and sweetheart love are both still in trouble."

It was funny —
Kirsty didn't think
of her parents as
sweethearts, but
she knew they
were. "Then we
have to look for
the rose first. I
don't like it
when my parents

argue," Kirsty confessed. "Especially on Valentine's Day."

Rachel paused. She had been hoping to look for the candy hearts first. She really wanted to make sure that friendship love was safe! But instead of fighting, she forced herself to smile. "Okay. Where should we start?"

First Stop: Florist

Kirsty led the way as the girls pedaled their bikes to the town square. They kept their eyes out for their new fairy friend. They hadn't seen Juliet since she'd taken the magic card back to Fairyland the day before!

Once they arrived in town, Rachel and Kirsty locked up their bikes and sat on a bench to eat their muffins. "How are we going to track down a single red rose?" Rachel asked between bites. "Lots of people send flowers on Valentine's Day."

"My dad always uses that florist," Kirsty said. She pointed to a small shop down the street.

It had an arched doorway covered in vines. The hand-painted sign in the window read FULL BLOOM FLOWERS.

Just then, the
florist's van
pulled up in
front of the
brick building.
"Let's hope
Juliet's flower
wasn't already
delivered to
someone," said

Rachel, brushing crumbs from her
winter coat.

"There's only one way to find out,"
Kirsty declared. She stood up and
headed toward the shop with Rachel
close behind. Just as they reached the
steps, a young man with short hair
and wire-rimmed glasses brushed past
them. He yanked on the door and

stepped inside. The door started to swing shut right in front of the girls.

"Oh!" the man yelped, catching the door just in time. "I'm sorry! I didn't mean to let it close. My mind is somewhere else."

"It's okay," Rachel
said. As she looked up
at the man's slender
face, she could see
that his eyes were sad.

Rachel nudged
Kirsty to make sure her
friend noticed, too.

Inside the shop, a woman with short
brown hair closed the sliding door to a
display case filled with colorful flowers.
"May I help you?" she asked. She held
a pair of stem cutters in one hand. Her
nametag read LILLIE.

"Yes," the young man said stepping
forward. "I need a red rose."

Kirsty and Rachel listened closely.
They needed a red rose, too!

Lillie bit her lip. "I'm sorry," she said, "but we don't have any red roses left. We haven't had them in stock all week. Luckily, we haven't received very many orders — but that's awfully strange at this time of year!"

The man shook his head in disbelief. "It's Valentine's Day! You have to help me," he said, clutching his hands together. "I tried to send red roses to

my sweetheart, but black ones were delivered instead. The note on the card was mixed up, too. It wasn't what I wrote at all. Now she thinks I don't want to be her sweetheart anymore." The man's hands shook.

Rachel and Kirsty looked at each other with concern. This sounded like the work of goblins! The girls knew that they were mixing up messages with Jack Frost's wand.

Lillie took a deep breath. "Let me see when we'll get more roses in," she said, turning to her computer. The keyboard clicked as her fingers tapped away. Then she looked up from the computer screen. "I'm very sorry, sir," she apologized. "I've been trying to order more roses from the local greenhouse all week, but the e-mails came back all scrambled. And no

one is answering the phone." Lillie
sighed. "Maybe you want some bright,
cheery tulips instead?"

"No, that won't do. I need a red rose,"
the man said sadly. His shoulders
drooped as he turned and walked out
the door.

"How awful!" Rachel said, turning to
Kirsty.

Kirsty nodded. "It's
also weird," she said.
"Why wouldn't the
greenhouse fill orders
for red roses on
Valentine's Day? I
think we need to visit
Greenhouse Gardens on the other side
of town." She walked quickly toward
the door.

Rachel stood in the same place, her brow furrowed. She was still thinking about the man and his sweetheart.

"Come on!" Kirsty called from the doorway, with one hand on her hip. At once, Rachel rushed to catch up with her friend.

Egg Sure Harden Nose?

Outside the florist, the girls hopped on their bikes. Kirsty zoomed out in front, leading the way. "There are really pretty gardens on the far side of Wetherbury," Kirsty yelled over the wind. "If anyone still has red roses, it's them."

Rachel nodded, working hard to pedal as fast as Kirsty. They left the town

square and headed down a narrow road
with tall trees lining both sides. Rachel
thought it was beautiful, but the ride was
taking a long time. She wondered if they
should have stayed in town and looked
for the magic box of candy hearts,
instead. Then, all at once, something up
ahead caught her eye. "Look at that
sign!" she called to Kirsty. "What does
it mean?"

Both girls slowed their bikes and examined the sign. "EGG SURE HARDEN NOSE," Kirsty murmured. "That's weird. I feel like I've seen this sign before, but with different words." The sign was made of wood, and the letters were bright green. In each corner was a simple painting of a red rose.

EGG SURE HARDEN NOSE. As she read it, Rachel couldn't help but touch

her nose to make sure it wasn't hard!

"It doesn't make any sense," she said. "They're real words, but it seems like they're all scrambled."

"That's it!" Kirsty cried. "I knew I had seen this sign before. It's supposed to read GREENHOUSE GARDENS. The goblins must have been here! They

EGG SURE HARDEN NOSE

used their wand to mix up the letters in
the sign." Kirsty jumped on her bike.
"We have to hurry — I bet the goblins
are already at the gardens!"

Rachel let out a long breath as she
watched Kirsty pedal away. Why was
her friend being so bossy? After all,
Rachel wanted to help Juliet, too.

Kirsty didn't look back as she
tore down the road toward the
gardens. In the back of her
mind, she wondered if
her parents were still
fighting. If she could
just find that rose, she
would feel a lot better!

She turned down a
gravel lane and saw
the first in a long line

of buildings with glass roofs. "The greenhouses," she whispered. When she noticed two gardeners by a fountain, she squeezed her brakes.

Kirsty glanced back and saw Rachel far down the lane. She propped her bike against a large tree trunk. "I'll just ask some questions," she said to herself, striding along the cobblestone path. The workers, who were both wearing overalls and thick gloves, seemed surprised to see her. "Excuse me," she began. "Do you have any red rosebushes that are still blooming?" The two gardeners looked at each other. "Why, we still have whole greenhouses full," one said. He had deep green eyes and leaned on a rake. "We

hardly got any orders
for red roses this year."

Kirsty couldn't
believe her ears! Lillie's
e-mails from the florist
must have been all
jumbled by the time they reached
the gardeners, thanks to those tricky
goblins.

"But a group of kids just bought all the
cut roses," the other gardener, who had
her hair tied back in a handkerchief,
explained. "It must be for some kind of
school project."

"Yeah, I saw them leaving the main
building. It looked like they all had green
thumbs!" the first gardener chimed in.
They both laughed.

Kirsty's eyes grew wide at the mention of green thumbs. "Thank you so much," she said quickly before racing back to her bike. Rachel was waiting for her there.

"The gardeners said that some kids with green thumbs bought all the cut roses!" Kirsty exclaimed, swinging her leg over the bike seat and placing her foot

on the pedal. "It must be the goblins —
let's go!"

"Kirsty," Rachel said calmly, "look
who's here." She smiled and pointed to
her shoulder. There sat Juliet! The little
fairy's head was lowered and her ankles
were crossed. Her wand dangled loosely
in her hand.

"Oh!" Kirsty replied, surprised to see
their fairy friend.
"Hi, Juliet. You're
just in time. We're
about to catch the
goblins!"

"I think it's going
to take a minute.
Juliet is feeling kind
of sad," Rachel
explained.

Kirsty glanced toward the main
building, and then looked at Juliet's pale
face. She took her foot off the bike pedal
and frowned. "Juliet, is there anything
we can do?" she asked.

A Glum Fairy

Juliet looked up at Rachel. "Can you explain to Kirsty?" she asked in a tiny voice.

Rachel nodded and lifted her chin. "Juliet is sad because no one is enjoying Valentine's Day," Rachel began. "Not only that, but people aren't being good friends or working together."

Kirsty looked at her friend and thought she saw a hint of a smile. She was sure that was Rachel trying to make a point. "Are you saying that I'm not being a good friend?" Kirsty asked, her voice getting higher. "I'm just trying to help!"

"You could have waited for me," Rachel responded quietly. "We always track down the goblins together!"

"It's not my fault that you can't bike as fast as I can," Kirsty shot back. "And it's not like you always think about my feelings. You gave my Valentine's card to the goblins!"

Suddenly, Juliet flew up from
Rachel's shoulder, shaking her head
and waving her arms. "No, no, no!"
she cried. "This is just what Jack Frost
wants! Please think of all the sweethearts
and friends who need your help," the
fairy begged.

Rachel and Kirsty stared at each other.
They both knew it was important to put

aside their differences and help Juliet, but it didn't make the bad feelings go away.

"This spell is strong," Juliet said, her eyes serious. "I can't stop Jack Frost's magic on my own."

A light wind blew down the lane and through the trees.

"We'll work together," Rachel said. "All of us."

Kirsty nodded firmly.

The color returned to Juliet's cheeks as she swooped down between the girls. "Let's shake on it," she said, reaching her small hand out in front of her. Kirsty quickly placed a finger on top of Juliet's hand, and then Rachel put her finger on top of Kirsty's.

The fairy grinned. "When best friends make a pact, may their friendship stay intact," she recited.

Kirsty waited for a burst of heart sparkles to leap from Juliet's wand, but nothing happened. "Was that magic?" she asked.

"Yes," Juliet replied. "The purest magic of all — true friendship." She smiled at Rachel and Kirsty. "With the two of you on my side, I know we can save Valentine's Day!"

Rachel and Kirsty smiled at each other.

"Well, we'd better get going," Rachel declared. "I think Kirsty was right. Those kids with green thumbs must be the goblins."

"Then what are we waiting for?" Juliet asked with a giggle.

"Let's go through this row of greenhouses," suggested Kirsty. "Maybe we can cut them off!" She climbed on

her bike and pedaled over the bumpy
cobblestone path, pausing to make sure
Rachel was right behind her.

As they came to a clearing, Kirsty
spotted the main building with its
beautiful Victorian house. She scanned
the paths for a sign of the goblins.

Juliet flitted off of Rachel's shoulder
and high into the air. After a quick
search, she let out a cry.

"There! Just over that hill!" she said, pointing. Kirsty and Rachel took off at once. From the top of the hill, they could see a band of goblins, all dressed like old-fashioned farmers with checked shirts, overalls, and straw hats. Each goblin had a wagon filled with pails of red roses.

"They look kind of sweet," said Rachel, watching the goblins pull the wagons down the steep, dusty hill.

"Sure, if you forget that they stole
Juliet's rose!" Kirsty said.

"And that they want to take it back to
Jack Frost," Juliet added.

"Well, that's true. So let's get them!"
Rachel declared, thrusting her fist into
the air. All at once, she lost her balance
and fell onto the handlebars, and her
bike rolled forward. A second later,
Rachel was barreling down the hill!

A Muddy Mess

"Help!" Rachel yelled as her bike sped faster and faster toward the bottom of the hill — and the goblins. A thick cloud of dust rose into the air behind her.

"What's that?" yelped the goblins, glancing up the hill. "Watch out!"

Kirsty dropped her bike. She ran after

Rachel. She could hardly see through all the dust in the air! Juliet flew right next to her. Kirsty's mind raced, trying to come up with a plan. "Run for your lives!" yelled a goblin. "Get out of the way!"

The goblins started to scramble in every direction, their wagons slamming into one another.

Suddenly, the screech of brakes rang through the air. With a giant *crash*, wagons tipped over

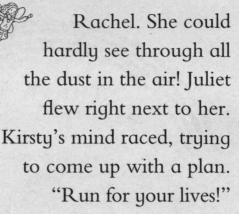

and pails of roses spilled onto the dirt path.

When the dust cleared, Kirsty was relieved to see that Rachel had landed in the soft grass. The goblins were not so lucky. They were in a muddy mess in the middle of the path.

"Something's pricking me!" a goblin with large feet screeched. "Yeouch!"

"Me, too," whined another goblin. "Silly, thorny roses."

Rachel stood up carefully and dusted off her knees, glancing over at the goblins.

Juliet fluttered over to make sure that Rachel wasn't hurt. Then she

quickly took shelter in the bike
basket, so the goblins wouldn't
see her.

Rachel and Kirsty
grinned at each other
as they listened to
the goblins whine
and moan. "Oh,
it hurts!" yelped
another one.
"Get those roses
off me!"

Just then, Kirsty
had an idea. "You
poor goblins," she
said, kneeling down
next to them. "Do you need
some help?"

"Oh, yes please. Get these horrible, thorny roses off of us!" they cried. "Of course," Kirsty kindly agreed. She delicately pulled the roses away one by one. She handed each rose to Rachel, who stood by her side. "It's too bad that these beautiful roses have so many thorns,"

Kirsty said, plucking
flowers from the
goblins' green skin.

When she came to
the last goblin, she
sighed sympathetically.
"This thorn in your

side looks very painful. Should I pull it out for you?"

"Of course," the goblin grumbled. As she gently reached for the rose, Kirsty spotted something dangling from its long stem: a sparkly red ribbon! Kirsty smiled with glee as she handed the rose to Rachel. Without a word, Rachel carried

it over to Juliet in the
bike basket. The
goblins were all too
busy moaning and
groaning to notice!

Kirsty pulled one
last thorn off the
goblin. "That's it," she
announced.

"Hey, don't I know
you?" the goblin asked, rubbing his side
and peering at Kirsty. "Wait! You're one
of those pesky girls!"

"Pesky?" Kirsty questioned. "I just
pulled thorns off you and all of your
friends. That doesn't seem very
pesky to me." Kirsty put her hands
on her hips.

"You weren't trying to steal Jack

Frost's rose?" the goblin asked, leaning so
close to Kirsty's face that his long nose
touched hers.

"Of course not!" Kirsty insisted. "I
would never steal something that
belonged to Jack Frost."

Kirsty chose her words carefully. She
didn't want to tell a lie, even to the
goblins. But the rose didn't belong to
Jack Frost. It belonged to Juliet!

The goblin squinted his eyes. "Fine,
then. You can go."

Kirsty took a deep breath. She'd gotten the magic rose back, but she needed one more thing. "Could I have just one rose? I'll let you choose which one I take." She bit her lip.

The goblin paused and looked over at his friends. They were all huddled together, arguing over whose cuts and scrapes were the worst. "Go ahead," one grumbled. "Those roses are a pain, anyway."

The goblin with the big feet bent down and reached for a beautiful red rose that was in full bloom. He brushed a speck of dirt from one of the leaves and handed the rose to Kirsty.

"Thank you," Kirsty said sweetly, nodding at the goblin.

She walked over to Rachel and dropped the rose gently in the bike basket. Rachel wheeled the bike next to her, and the girls headed up the hill together before the goblins had time to notice that the magic rose had disappeared.

"Juliet already went back to Fairyland with the magic rose," Rachel whispered. "She thought it was the safest thing to do. She said to tell you an extra-special thank you."

Kirsty smiled at her best friend. "Is it okay if we head back to the town square now?"

"Oh yes," agreed Rachel. "We should tell Lillie that there are plenty more red roses for the shop."

"And we know someone who wanted just one rose," said Kirsty, thinking of the man who had visited the florist that morning. As the girls looked at the single rose in the bike basket, magical red and pink hearts swirled around the petals. When they disappeared, the flower

seemed to glow. It was even more beautiful than before. Sweetheart love was safe again!

"I can't wait to give this rose to him," Kirsty said. She grinned at Rachel. "I think it's going to be a very happy Valentine's Day, after all!"

The Candy Heart Compromise

Contents

Loose Ends

"The magical red rose must be back in Fairyland by now," Rachel Walker guessed, glancing around the town square. "There are couples everywhere!"

Rachel's best friend, Kirsty Tate, nodded. It was the afternoon of Valentine's Day, and people were walking their dogs, flying kites, and drinking coffee — two by two. Couples held hands and laughed. Sweetheart love was blooming all around Wetherbury!

"Now we just have one more Valentine's present to find," Kirsty said, watching as two workers put up a stage in the center of the grassy square.

"The box of candy hearts," Rachel added. The final present was especially important to Kirsty and Rachel. After

all, the candy hearts stood for the love between friends! Juliet the Valentine Fairy needed to get the box of candy hearts back to Fairyland right away. It was the only way to make sure that friendship love was safe from Jack Frost.

Kirsty and Rachel knew just how strong Jack Frost's magic could be. Even though they were best friends, they had been arguing with each other — a lot.

"I don't have a clue where we should start looking," admitted Rachel.

"Then let's tie up some loose ends. We can go to

Full Bloom Flowers and talk to Lillie," Kirsty suggested. "We'll tell her that there are a lot more red roses at Greenhouse Gardens, if she needs them."

"That's a good plan," Rachel agreed. "Maybe the magic will come to us while we're there!"

As the girls headed across the town square, Kirsty

carefully carried the single red rose from Greenhouse Gardens. It was beautiful. She could hardly wait to give it to the man with the wire-rimmed glasses that they'd met earlier in the day. When the friends entered the flower shop, it seemed like a different place. The store was crowded with customers, and the phone was ringing nonstop. Lillie was wrapping a large bouquet behind the counter. "Here are your daisies," she said to an older man with a feather in his cap. "She'll love them." Kirsty and Rachel looked at a nearby display case. It was empty! They hurried to the counter.

"Excuse me," Kirsty said.

Lillie looked up, and her jaw dropped. "A red rose," she whispered. "Where did you get it?"

"We just came from Greenhouse Gardens," Rachel told the florist. "They should have plenty more to send your way."

"Really?" Lillie questioned. "That's wonderful, but I haven't been able to

reach the greenhouse by
e-mail or phone."

Rachel looked
at Kirsty. How
could they
explain that
those problems
had disappeared
as soon as Juliet
returned the

red rose to Fairyland? "Maybe you
should give it one more try," Rachel
suggested.

Lillie looked first at her empty display
case and then at all the customers in
the shop. She reached for the phone
and crossed her fingers. After a minute,
Lillie's eyebrows raised. "Gwen? I've
been trying to reach you all week!" She

paused. "Absolutely! I'll take them all." Lillie smiled as she hung up the phone. "Thank you so much!" she gushed to Rachel and Kirsty.

"Of course," Rachel said, smiling.

"Happy Valentine's Day!" Kirsty added. The girls waved before walking out the door and down the shop's steps.

The sun was bright, and Kirsty lifted one hand to shield her eyes. In the other, she still clutched the red rose.

"Oh! Look who I see!" Rachel cried, pointing up ahead.

As Kirsty scanned the town square, she felt something slip through her fingers. Rachel had taken the rose! The next thing Kirsty knew, her friend was running across the street. Kirsty rushed after her, but by the time she reached the

crosswalk, the light was red and she had to stop.

She watched Rachel stride toward a wooden bench — right up to the man with the wire-rimmed glasses!

Best Friends Bicker

Kirsty bit her lip. She couldn't believe that Rachel had taken the rose right out of her hand!

From across the street, she could see Rachel talking to the young man. His face lit up. He took the rose from Rachel and gave her a quick hug before rushing off, practically skipping across the square.

 Just then, a flurry
of fairy dust fell on
Kirsty's nose. She
looked up to see
Juliet fluttering
overhead.
The tiny fairy
darted to Kirsty's
shoulder and ducked under her scarf.

"Kirsty, I'm sorry," Juliet said softly.
"I saw the whole thing. But you know
Rachel didn't mean to hurt your
feelings, right?"

Kirsty heard the fairy's kind voice and
nodded, but her feelings were still hurt.
She suddenly realized that Jack Frost's
magic must be even worse for other
people. They didn't know that the

goblins were mixing up messages, or that
Jack Frost's spell was keeping friends
from getting along. How horrible!

"We'll find the magic candy hearts.
We can do it if we all work together,"
Juliet vowed.

The crosswalk light changed, and Kirsty headed across the street. Rachel ran to meet her.

"He was so excited!" Rachel exclaimed, clapping her hands. "He said it was the most beautiful rose ever. He couldn't wait to give it to his girlfriend. I wish you could have seen his face."

"Yeah, I do, too," mumbled Kirsty, looking down.

"What?" Rachel asked, leaning closer. "Sorry that you missed it."

Kirsty shrugged. "Juliet's here," she said, changing the subject. Kirsty tilted her head so Juliet could peek out from beneath her scarf. The fairy gave Rachel a small smile.

"Hi, Juliet!" Rachel said brightly. "Sweetheart love is safe. Now we can focus on finding the last Valentine present."

"Rachel?" Juliet's voice was quiet. "Did you know that Kirsty wanted to give the man the rose, too?"

Rachel paused. "I hadn't really thought about it," she admitted.

"I wish you had waited for me,"
Kirsty said, looking down at her shoes.
"Everything is more fun when we do it
together."

"It's not a big deal," said Rachel with
a shrug. "We can find the candy hearts
together now."

"Okay," Kirsty said, feeling a little
better. "How about we check out all the
stores that sell candy? There's Poppy's

Gifts, The Sweet Shop, and Mr. Baxter's Market."

Rachel sighed. "Why can't we just let the magic come to us? Let's stay here and watch the Valentine's Day Pageant."

The workers had finished putting up the stage. Now they were placing chairs in rows for the audience. Families were beginning to arrive.

All at once, Juliet and the girls heard an awful screech. They turned to see two boys tugging at a scooter. There was another scream as two girls nearby fought over a pair of heart-shaped sunglasses. In fact, when the three friends glanced around, they saw small groups of kids quarreling everywhere!

"All of those best friends are fighting," Juliet worried.

"We can't just stay here," Kirsty insisted. "We have to find the candy hearts fast!"

"Okay," huffed Rachel. "But I have to go to the bathroom first — and I think

138

Juliet should come with me. She isn't
hidden well enough on your shoulder.
Someone could see her!"

It was true. Juliet could hide better
behind Rachel's long hair, but she
obviously felt bad leaving Kirsty.

"You should go," Kirsty said to the
fairy. "I'll stay on the lookout here. We
can meet by the bikes."

Juliet flitted over to Rachel's
shoulder and waved.

Kirsty headed toward
where she and Rachel
had locked their bikes.
Suddenly, she gasped.
She searched for a pen
and paper and quickly
scrawled out a note for
Rachel.

THE GOBLINS ARE HERE!

IN THE SQUARE!

WE'LL FIND THOSE CANDY HEARTS YET!

When Rachel and Juliet came back a few minutes later, Kirsty was not by the bikes. They didn't see their friend anywhere!

One More Mixed-up Message

"I thought she told us to meet her by the bikes," said Rachel, peering around the square. "I hope she didn't go off on her own again." Rachel didn't really want to hunt all over town for the candy, but she also didn't want Kirsty to do it without her!

"Look!" Juliet cried from her perch on Rachel's shoulder. "In the bike basket!"

Rachel reached into the straw basket and pulled out a piece of paper. When she unfolded it, she saw a note in Kirsty's handwriting.

I WILL FIND THE CANDY HEARTS!
SEE THE TEAL QUEENS!
HEAR NO BERRY GHOST!

Rachel read the note again and again. The last two lines didn't make any sense, but the first line upset her. "I can't believe that Kirsty went to find the candy by herself!" Rachel pouted. "Do you think she's still upset about the red rose?"

"I don't think so," Juliet replied, giving her head a small shake. "She understands that a lot of things are mixed up because of Jack Frost's magic."

Rachel sighed. "I'm tired of bickering best friends and mixed-up messages," she muttered.

"Mixed-up messages!" Juliet gasped. "Let's read that note again!" Rachel held

the paper up so Juliet could see it. "The last two lines make no sense," the little fairy said.

"It seems like they're scrambled," Rachel agreed. "Just like the sign to Greenhouse Gardens!" She took a deep breath and looked around the square.

"But why would Kirsty have run off and only left a note?" Juliet wondered.

"Because of the goblins!" said Rachel. Juliet followed Rachel's gaze to see a flash of green near the stage. "They must have mixed up Kirsty's note with their wand," Rachel guessed. "I'll bet she wrote the note to warn us about the goblins. Then she had to hide from them."

"We should find her," Juliet said. "And if the goblins are here, I'll bet the magical candy hearts are close by, too!"

Just then, a boy stepped onto the stage at the center of the square.  He looked like he was about seven years old, and he seemed nervous. "Welcome to Evening Street School's Valentine's Day Pageant," he said, standing on his tiptoes to reach the microphone. "Mrs. Bowlus will lead

the second-grade choir in songs, and Mr.
Barrymore will direct the dancers."

The boy let out a sigh of relief, and a
woman with short, curly hair led a group
of children onto the stage. They walked
in a long line and wore red and pink
shirts. The audience clapped loudly. Next
a tall, thin man stepped on the stage,

followed by girls wearing white shirts,
wispy skirts, and ballet shoes. Finally,
a group of boys dressed like Cupid
appeared. After the graceful dancers,
they seemed clumsy with their big feet
clomping on the stage.

"Hmmm," Juliet murmured. "Do they
really need seven boys to play Cupid?"

"It's very strange," Rachel agreed. "And why are they . . . *green*?" Then she and Juliet looked a little closer. They burst into laughter. The boys dressed as Cupid — and wearing little more than diapers — were the goblins!

Cupids and Candy

Rachel and Juliet watched the stage closely. The singers, dancers, and goblins were all elbowing one another and frowning.

"No one is getting along!" Juliet sighed. Rachel turned and looked at the fairy perched on her shoulder. Juliet seemed tired . . . and sad.

Rachel and Juliet watched as Mr. Barrymore, the dance teacher, tried to direct the show. The goblins were not only bumping into one another, but they even knocked over one of the ballet dancers! Each time one of the goblins made a mistake, the others grumbled and scowled at him.

"They're horrible," Rachel admitted, "but the audience thinks they're funny."

The people in the audience laughed as the goblins tried to leap through the air while holding large hearts made of red construction paper.

"Those Cupids are hilarious," said a man sitting in the back row. He put his hand on his belly as he chuckled.

"Well, at least the pageant is keeping the goblins busy," Juliet pointed out. "This is our chance to find Kirsty and the candy hearts!"

Rachel took off, jogging around the growing crowd. The choir began singing "All You Need Is Love," and the audience joined in. Rachel passed the

bandstand and then
stopped to peek around
the back corner of the
stage. At once, she saw
Kirsty. Her best friend
was elbow-
deep in large
shopping
bags full of
candy heart boxes.

Rachel was about to join Kirsty
when she saw something move on the far
side of the bandstand. The goblins!

"Kirsty," Rachel whispered
loudly, trying to alert her. "Kirsty!"

Kirsty looked up, delighted to see
her friend. She waved for Rachel to
join her.

"Watch out!" Rachel yelled, pointing to the line of goblins coming around the back of the stage. Kirsty glanced over her shoulder and immediately straightened up. She darted off behind a hot dog cart.

The best friends exchanged worried glances from afar as they watched the

goblins scurry over to the bags of candy.
"Come on, you slowpokes!" demanded a
long-nosed goblin. "We have to hurry.
The magic candy hearts are in here
somewhere!"

"You're not the boss!"
argued the goblin with
extremely large feet.
"We don't have to
listen to you."

"Why is everyone
whining and yelling?"
cried the goblin who
had given Kirsty the
red rose at the
gardens. "You're all
annoying me more
than usual!"

Just then, Mr. Barrymore appeared backstage. "Cupids, there you are," he announced. "The pageant is almost over. It's time to hand out the candy hearts to the audience."

"But we were just —" began the long-nosed goblin.

"No buts," Mr. Barrymore declared. "It's Valentine's Day. Now go give

those boxes of candy to the crowd! All of you."

The goblins glared at one another. They each picked up a bag and trudged off, grumbling all the way.

Goblin Goodies

Kirsty and Rachel watched the goblins head into the audience with the bags of candy hearts in tow. Both girls ran into the crowd, chasing different goblins and hoping to spot the box with the sparkly red ribbon. Juliet stayed hidden on Rachel's shoulder, so no one would spot her.

After a few minutes, Kirsty spotted Rachel across the square and caught her eye. Rachel frowned and shook her head. Kirsty did the same. Neither one of them had found the magic candy yet!

Kirsty was dizzy and tired from

racing around and scanning the crowd. Then, out of the corner of her eye, she saw a flash of green dashing toward the other side of the square. Kirsty raced after it as fast as she could. "Wait!" she called. "Please wait! I need your help!" Kirsty was surprised when the goblin skidded to a stop.

"You need my help?" the goblin questioned.

Kirsty nodded, recognizing him as the goblin who had given her the rose. He seemed to recognize her, too. "I think you have something I need." As she said it, she peeked into the goblin's bag and glimpsed a sparkle of red.

"But I need it, too," said the goblin. "Why should I give it to you?"

"Well," Kirsty began, "the truth is, it's not for me. I want to give it to my best friend. Ever since the magic presents went missing, we've been arguing. I hope that if I give her the candy hearts, things will go back to normal."

The goblin looked Kirsty in the eye. He reached into his bag and pulled out the box. The red ribbon shimmered

in the afternoon sun. "You think these hearts will magically make you friends again?" he asked.

Kirsty paused. "We're still friends," she tried to explain. "But I think the hearts will help us remember how important our friendship is. See how the hearts all have friendship phrases on them? This one says FRIENDS FOREVER, and this one says BEST BUDS."

The goblin bit his lip, and his chin trembled. Then, to Kirsty's surprise, he began to sob! "My friends and I have been fighting, too!" he cried. "I want to give them candy hearts. I want them to remember that we're best buds!"

Kirsty quickly searched her pockets and handed the goblin a tissue. He blew his

nose, which
blared like
a trombone.
She put her
hand on the
goblin's shoulder.
"I think I can
help you," she assured
him. "Have a seat on this
bench. I'll be right back."

Kirsty headed into the crowd again,
searching for Rachel and Juliet. When
she found them, she told them her plan.
They all rushed back to the bench,
and the goblin greeted them with a
hopeful smile.

"Juliet has something for you," Kirsty
said. With a whirl of her wand, Juliet

created six small boxes of candy hearts.
Each box was shaped like a big heart!
They gently floated down and landed on
the bench next to the goblin.

"If you let us have Juliet's magical
candy hearts, you can have these —

there's a box for each of your friends,"
Rachel explained.

The goblin still clutched the magical
candy in his hands. He leaned over
and looked at the candy hearts Juliet
had made.

"THE GOBLIN
GANG," he
read aloud
from one
piece of candy.
"GREEN IS
GREAT." A
smile spread
across his face. "It's a deal!" He

hastily placed the magical candy
hearts in Rachel's hand. "Your friend
wanted to give these to you," he said.
Then he gathered the six boxes in his

arms and scurried off toward the
stage.

Rachel, Kirsty, and Juliet all cheered.
"Soon all friends will be able to truly
celebrate Valentine's Day, thanks to both
of you," Juliet said. When Rachel
handed the box with the sparkly red

ribbon to Juliet, it immediately shrunk to Fairyland-size. "Off I go!" Juliet exclaimed with a wide grin. She disappeared in a twinkling of heart-shaped sparkles.

Kirsty and Rachel both let out big sighs of relief and sank down on the park bench. "I've never been so happy to see a fairy return to Fairyland," Rachel said.

"It's hard to believe, but I think the goblins are glad, too," Kirsty said. She pointed across the square to where

the whole gang was sitting in a circle,
reading and eating candy hearts.

"And we can't forget all the happy
sweethearts," Rachel said, pointing to
a couple walking and looking dreamily
into each other's eyes.

"That's my parents!" Kirsty realized,
a blush coloring her cheeks. Rachel
giggled.

All at once, there was a burst of sparkles, and a red, heart-shaped velvet box appeared on the bench between the girls. Rachel and Kirsty opened the box together. Inside was a handwritten note.

Thank you for being such good friends.
    Love,
    Juliet

Under the note, the girls found two matching heart-shaped lockets that read FAIRY FRIENDS FOREVER. They took turns

putting the necklaces on each other.
"They're beautiful," Kirsty said.

"Yes,"
Rachel
agreed,
linking arms
with Kirsty.
"They really
are." The
girls were

ready to share the rest of Valentine's
Day together — like true best friends!

RAINBOW
magic™
SPECIAL EDITION

Don't miss Rachel and Kirsty's other
magical adventures! Join them for more
sweet, sparkly fun as they help

Mia
the Bridesmaid Fairy!

Take a look at this special
sneak peek. . . .

Wedding Plans

"Isn't it exciting that we're going to be Esther's bridesmaids?" Rachel Walker said happily.

"Yes — I can hardly wait for next Saturday!" replied Kirsty Tate, smiling at her best friend. "And it'll be twice as much fun with you here!"

The girls were in Kenbury, the pretty
little village where Kirsty's cousin Esther
had grown up. The sun was shining
brightly and there wasn't a cloud in the
sky. It was perfect wedding weather!

Esther, Mrs. Tate, and Aunt Isabel,
Esther's mom, were in the nearby
wedding dress store. The girls had popped
outside to look at the pretty church
where Esther was going to get married.

"Oh, Kirsty, look!" cried Rachel.
"There must be a wedding today!"

People were arriving in their best
clothes, carrying cameras and little boxes
of confetti.

A cream-colored car pulled up in front
of the church, and a chauffeur jumped
out and opened the back door. Inside,

the girls could see a woman wearing a beautiful white dress.

"It's the bride!" Rachel exclaimed as she and Kirsty walked back to the wedding store.

"I love the dress in the window!" said Kirsty.

"Me, too," Rachel agreed.

Under an archway of roses, an exquisite wedding dress was surrounded by handfuls of real flowers.

"Bella's an amazing dressmaker!" Kirsty said, with a happy sigh.

Just then, Aunt Isabel popped her head out of the store's front door.

"Girls, come back inside," she said with a beaming smile. "Bella is ready for you to try on your dresses."

Rachel and Kirsty hurried to the room at the back of the store. Bella held up two amazing dresses, and the girls' eyes widened.

"Oh, they're beautiful!" Rachel whispered.

The two best friends quickly got changed, giggling with excitement. Then they stood in front of the long mirror.

"Oh, girls, you look fabulous!" cried Aunt Isabel.

"Just like princesses!" Esther added.

The dresses were pale blue, and they shimmered and sparkled with hundreds of tiny silver beads. Soft frills made the gowns swirl around the girls' legs, and the sleeves were made from fine blue silk. They fluttered when the girls moved their arms.

"They're just like fairy wings!" Kirsty whispered to Rachel.

Bella checked that the dresses fit properly, and made some small alterations.

"Thank you, girls," she said eventually. "You can get changed now."

"Our dresses are just gorgeous," sighed Rachel, smiling at Bella. "We love the one in the window, too. Is it waiting to be picked up?"

"No," said Bella. "It's a copy of one of my favorites, which I made a long time ago. I just couldn't bear to part with it, so I made another!"

"Wow, you must have made hundreds of dresses," said Aunt Isabel. "And I bet you know everything there is to know about weddings!"

"I've learned an awful lot," agreed Bella. "I love all the old traditions, and bridesmaids are one of the oldest traditions of all! It's their job to help everything go smoothly for the bride."

Rachel and Kirsty exchanged happy looks.

"What other wedding traditions are there?" Rachel asked.

"Do you know what a bride is supposed to carry up the aisle to bring her luck?" asked Bella. " 'Something old, something new, something borrowed, something blue, and a penny in her shoe'."

"There's nothing wrong with a little extra luck," said Esther, who had been trying on tiaras in front of the mirror.

"Girls, will you be in charge of finding me those four 'somethings' and a penny?"

"We'd love to!" Rachel said eagerly.

"Oh look, Rachel!" Kirsty exclaimed. "Let's start by looking over there!"

At the front of the store, along the window, was a low table filled with wedding accessories.

The girls dashed over to it, while Mrs. Tate, Esther, and Aunt Isabel stayed at the back of the store.

"Look at these little bride and groom figures," said Kirsty. "They must go on the top of wedding cakes!"

"And here's a little bridesmaid figure!" cried Rachel in delight. "Oh, Kirsty, I can't wait to be a bridesmaid!"

"Me neither," Kirsty agreed.

"How about if Esther borrows the pretty dragonfly pin your mom's wearing for the 'something old'?" Rachel suggested.

"That's perfect!" agreed Kirsty. "It's been in the family for years, so it's definitely old enough! Now we just have to think of something new, something borrowed, and something blue."

"And the penny for her shoe," Rachel reminded her. "Oh, Kirsty, look!"

She gave her best friend a nudge that made her squeak in surprise. The bridesmaid figure on the table had started to glow!

RAINBOW magic™

There's Magic in Every Series!

The Rainbow Fairies
The Weather Fairies
The Jewel Fairies
The Pet Fairies
The Fun Day Fairies
The Petal Fairies
The Dance Fairies
The Music Fairies
The Sports Fairies
The Party Fairies
The Ocean Fairies

Read them all!

SCHOLASTIC

www.scholastic.com
www.rainbowmagiconline.com

RMFAIRY3

RAINBOW magic

These activities are magical!

Play dress-up, send friendship notes, and much more!

SCHOLASTIC
www.scholastic.com
www.rainbowmagiconline.com

HiT entertainment

RMACTIV2